Elepop

Written by **Matilda Rose** • Illustrated by **Tim Budgen**

Sparkle
Castle

Rainbow
Lake

Twinkle
Castle

Fable
Fort

Coral Cove

Lighthouse
Lagoon

The Crystal
Mountains

Dragon
Vale

Enchanted
Forest

Princess Ava's
Palace

Fairy Toadstool
Village

Twinkleton-Under-
Beanstalk

Galloping Gala
Fields

N
W   E
S

Next time you're in Fairyland, make sure you visit Mrs Paws'
Magic Pet Shop in the town of Twinkleton-Under-Beanstalk.
It's truly an enchanting place. There are mystical meerkats,
glittering guinea pigs and playful pugicorns!

One day, Princess Ivy came to The Magic Pet
Shop to collect a special delivery.

fairy
Bakes

"Hello, Princess Ivy!" said Mrs Paws.
"Are you excited to meet your new pet?
She's VERY excited to meet you!"

Princess Ivy *was* feeling excited,
but she was also very worried.

The
Magic
Pet Shop

What if I can't look after her? What if my pet really, really doesn't like me?! Ivy wanted to say.

Instead, she simply smiled and said, "Can't wait!"

Then Mrs Paws clicked her fingers and out popped . . .

"Oh, she's perfect!" said Princess Ivy, forgetting her worries.

Elepop blew lots of rainbow bubbles from her trunk in delight!

That afternoon, Princess Ivy and Elepop had the most magical time.
They shared a banana split at the Ice Queen Parlour . . .

splashed around at Rainbow Lake . . .

scored strikes at Fairylanes Bowling . . .

and cosied up with a story at the Twinkleton Library.

On the way home, they bumped into Princess Ava and her pet, Pugicorn.

"Hi, Ivy!" said Ava, handing her a flyer. "Will you come along?"

The Magical Pet Parade!

CARNIVAL

For Twinkleton's princes, princesses and perfect pets.

Twinkleton Town Centre, Saturday, 12pm
Wear your best carnival costumes!

As Princess Ivy read the words, she felt worries bubbling up in her tummy. At the very same moment, Elepop's colourful bubbles turned red!

There isn't enough time to prepare! What if my costume isn't good enough?! Ivy wanted to shout.

Instead, she simply smiled and said, "Yes. Can't wait!"

All evening, Princess Ivy's tummy bubbled with worries about the pet parade . . . and more red bubbles popped out from Elepop's trunk!

"We definitely can't join the pet parade *now*, Elepop," said Ivy. "I've broken you!"

Elepop gave Ivy a big hug. Ivy hoped the colourful rainbow bubbles would come back – but they didn't.

The next morning was crafting club.

Princess Ivy's tummy swirled when she saw everyone preparing for the parade.

"We'll join in with the crafting," said Ivy in a wobbly voice, "though Elepop and I won't be going to the parade."

But Elepop's big red bubbles got in the way as Ivy tried to paint . . .

and as she counted threads for her dreamcatcher . . .

But they didn't get in the way of Elepop making friends!

"*Please* come to the pet parade, Ivy!" said Prince Miles.
"Elepop looks so great in a costume!"

What if Elepop's big red bubbles get in the way?
It's not a *broken* pet parade! Ivy wanted to cry.

Instead, she simply smiled and said, "Oh, alright then. I'll come!"

As they walked home, Princess Ivy's
worries were still bubbling in her tummy.

"Hello, Princess Ivy!" called Miss Green
as they passed Twinkleton Gardens.
"Are you alright?"

Ivy's fears swirled. She almost said, "I'm fine," . . . but then she spotted colourful bubbles floating around the gardens!

And there, next to Miss Green was . . .

. . . a pet just like hers!

"Why don't you help me and Nellypop plant these
flowers?" Miss Green suggested. "We can have a nice
chat – those red bubbles look bothersome!"

"Well, it all began when. . ." started Ivy, and soon she was telling Miss Green all about Elepop and the pet parade.

Ivy talked so much that she didn't even notice the red bubbles floating up and . . .

. . . popping in the sky!

"Elepop isn't broken," said Miss Green. "She's showing you that you can't ignore your feelings! Sometimes, sharing our worries can make them feel lighter."

Princess Ivy let out a huge sigh of relief. "I'm sorry, Elepop," she said. "I didn't realise you were trying to help!"

Elepop smiled and blew a big, bright rainbow bubble.

When the morning of the parade arrived, Ivy felt a little pang of worry. Suddenly, Elepop popped out a few red bubbles.

"I feel nervous about getting
dressed up, Elepop," Princess Ivy admitted.
And the red bubbles popped and changed colour!
Ivy smiled – she felt better after sharing.

The parade was nothing short of magical!
Princess Ivy had so much fun, and Elepop's
magical rainbow bubbles filled the air.

Later, Princess Ivy went to thank Miss Green.

"Thank our wonderful, magical pets!" Miss Green replied. "I would have never learned to share my worries if it weren't for Nellypop."

Now Princess Ivy knew exactly what to do if she ever felt a big red bubble of worry. And she'd always have a friend to talk to . . .

Elepop! Her perfect pet.

For Katie and Katie x
M.R.

To K.N., who loves elephants x
T.B.

HODDER CHILDREN'S BOOKS

First published in Great Britain in 2023
by Hodder and Stoughton

© Hodder & Stoughton Limited, 2023
Illustrations by Tim Budgen

A CIP catalogue record for this book is available from the British Library.

ISBN: 978 1 44496 648 0

1 3 5 7 9 10 8 6 4 2

Printed and bound in China

Hodder Children's Books
An imprint of Hachette Children's Group
Part of Hodder and Stoughton Limited
Carmelite House, 50 Victoria Embankment, London, EC4Y 0DZ

An Hachette UK Company
www.hachette.co.uk
www.hachettechildrens.co.uk